BORROWED

HOPE

Sarah's Story:

Triumph Over Infertility

Evangeline Colbert

Angela Williams

This is a work of creative nonfiction. Some parts have been fictionalized in varying degrees, for various purposes.

Borrowed Hope – Sarah's Story
Published by iHope Publishing
Copyright © 2015 by Evangeline Colbert and Angela Williams

Cover Art by Yoram Raanan -www.yoramraanan.com

ISBN: 978-0-9858303-5-9

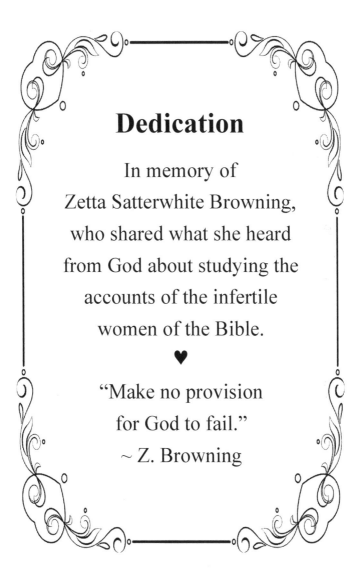

Dedication

In memory of
Zetta Satterwhite Browning,
who shared what she heard
from God about studying the
accounts of the infertile
women of the Bible.

♥

"Make no provision
for God to fail."
~ Z. Browning

"The Scriptures say that Abraham had two sons, one from his slave wife and one from his freeborn wife. The son of the slave wife was born in a human attempt to bring about the fulfillment of God's promise. But the son of the freeborn wife was born as God's own fulfillment of His promise."
Galatians 4:22-23 NLT

Introduction

God loves to make a way out of no way. He
created the universe from nothing, He caused
the shoes of the Israelites to last through forty
years of wandering in the desert, and He raised
the dead. He's "made a way" so many times—
they're innumerable to count! The good news is
that infertility was included in the Bible several
times as God made possible what seemed to be
impossible.

One couple that experienced His power to
overcome infertility was Abram and Sarai,
better known as Abraham and Sarah. Sarah
longed for a child but was unable to get
pregnant from the start of their marriage.
Decades of their lives had been filled with
monthly disappointments because Sarah was
not pregnant.

In *Sarah's Story*, perhaps you will notice
how Sarah experienced the same emotions that

you are possibly feeling. You will see how she moved from fear to doubt and anger but then began to have hope, faith, and eventually experienced victory.

We invite you to witness conversations that this couple likely had in their long season of infertility. Husbands and wives of today may have very similar conversations since the emotions of the infertility struggle remain the same as what Abraham and Sarah experienced.

This is their story of how they had hope in the midst of their season of waiting. *Sarah's Story* will encourage you and allow you to borrow hope from an overcomer when you feel as if you've lost yours.

Be sure to read the account at the end of this book of *a modern-day infertility overcomer* who borrowed hope from the Bible's descriptions of victory experienced by Sarah and other women with waiting wombs.

Profile of Sarah

An Infertility Overcomer

Sarah, the wife of Abraham, had an important role in God's covenant. She was to be the only one who would bear the *true* heir, the child God had promised to Abraham. During her infertility, God intervened many times to protect her so that His promise could be fulfilled. But her doubt and unbelief in God's faithfulness to His promise caused her to compromise and give another woman to her husband in order to birth a child. God's ultimate response was a question to Sarah, "Is anything too hard for the Lord?"

The scriptures only tell us of God's conversations with Abraham up to this point. Once Sarah heard God voice His opinion about her lack of trust in His willingness to have *her* birth Abraham's heir of promise, she concluded that He was indeed faithful to do what He had said. She finally understood that she didn't need to help God. She found assurance in knowing that not only was He able to stop the barrenness that she had experienced for decades, but that He was also extremely *willing* to manifest His promise.

Even though Sarah interfered with and attempted to manipulate God's plan, His loving-kindness and unmerited favor ensured that the child of promise would be born in God's timing and in His way.

 # Hope Notes

As you receive encouragement from Sarah's Story, you might find it helpful to record your revelations and new insights. Write them on the *HOPE NOTES* pages in the back of this book.

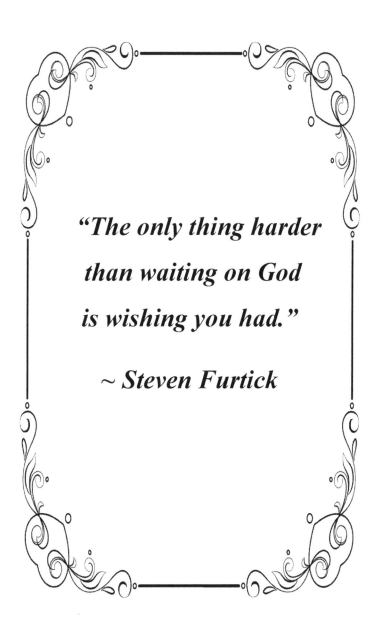

"The only thing harder than waiting on God is wishing you had."

~ Steven Furtick

FEAR

"The LORD had said to Abram, "Leave your native country, your relatives, and your father's family, and go to the land that I will show you."
Genesis 12:1 NLT

The first thing we learn about Sarai is that she was the wife of Abram *and* she was barren. In their society, women were considered cursed if they couldn't conceive. Initially, we're not told how she dealt with the pain and frustration of this struggle. One can only imagine that she experienced shame and fear in a culture and time where having a biological heir was of the utmost importance.

God chose Abram, knowing that He could trust him. Abram was set apart to be God's instrument to bless all the families of the world. Because of Abram's obedience, God singled him out from among his superstitious and idol-worshiping friends and family in the land of Haran. His extended family must have been a constant temptation to him. He could not live with them without being affected and *infected* by their idolatry.

The test for Abram, since he loved God, was whether or not he could willingly leave everything and everyone behind to go forward with God.

Abram and Sarai cut ties with their land, their people, and their home, and then cleaved only to the Lord, following as He directed. They had to leave everything they were accustomed to in order to rely only on God and to reap the benefits of His promises and grace. They would experience great gain by making this change in their lives.

Sarai felt lonely, scared, and unsure of herself, not knowing what she would face. She was leaving the comfort zone of family, friends, and community for an uncertain destination and future, all because her husband had "heard from God."

She must have wondered how she, being barren, and Abram, being old, could ever expect a lineage to come from them. Little did she know that what lay ahead of her would be the answer to her decades-long prayers about giving birth to a child. And not just any child—he would be the beginning of a nation that would produce blessings and a Savior for the entire world!

This is where we find Sarai in the story, questioning her life with Abram and ultimately, her destiny.

"So, God has told you to leave your father's family, your relatives, your native country? Really, Abram, why would that be so?" As she questioned Abram, Sarai found herself thinking about the huge task of packing up and preparing to leave her home. Since Terah, who was Abram's father, had passed away, Abram was now in charge and today he received new instructions from God.

"He's going to make me into a great nation," Abram said with pride. "He said He will bless me and make me famous. I will be a blessing to others and those who bless me will be blessed and those who treat me with contempt will be cursed. Me, Sarai; He was talking to me as sure as you're standing there!"

"And why would He do that, Abram? I think the world of you, but what makes you so special to God?"

"I don't know, Sarai, but He said it. It was clear and it made so much sense when He was telling me," Abram said with confidence.

"But Abram, you don't have any sons. How could this be so? You know I am barren and my womb is cursed. Yet the Almighty God is calling you blessed? He said that you, without any children, would be a mighty nation? How could that be so?"

"I don't know, Sarai, but God said it and so we must go." He glanced back and looked at Sarai with unwavering eyes, "We must go!"

"Yes, Abram, we must go," Sarai muttered to herself. With fear and uncertainty, Sarai considered life without family. She had not heard Abram's conversation with God and didn't know the details. Her mind was filled with many questions: *What exactly was God going to do? How was God going to bring children forth for Abram and what would her role be in all of this? Was God going to give*

Abram a different wife? It did not make any sense to Sarai, but she did not have time to figure it out. She threw up her hands in surrender and began to pack.

When Abram left the tent, he headed out to the fields where Lot was working. Lot was the only member of the family that Abram allowed to come along, as God had instructed Abram to leave his relatives and his father's family and go where God would send him. Lot was part of the entourage that would leave the city of Haran with Abram and Sarai. Excited about all he heard from the Lord, Abram began to explain to Lot what God had revealed.

"Where are we headed, Abram?" asked Lot.

"We're headed to Canaan," Abram replied.

"Isn't that where your father, Terah, was headed when we first left Ur?"

"Yes it is, Lot."

Abram paused as he fondly thought of his father. What a wise man Terah was. He loved

Abram and he loved his grandson, Lot, who was Haran's boy. Haran had died and Terah had taken on the father role for Lot. Now that Haran and Terah were both gone, Abram assumed that role.

Abram was very fond of Lot and reminisced with him.

"I'm sorry my father did not get to set out with us and reach Canaan. But I'm sure he'd want us to go to the place God had told him about all those years ago." The memory of Terah's decision to go to Canaan encouraged Abram's heart and made him think that Canaan must be a special place.

Abram, Sarai, Lot and all the men, women and children whom he had taken into his household in Haran, traveled to Canaan and set up camp beside the oak of Moreh. They also took all the livestock that Abram owned.

Sarai managed the household and kept things running smoothly as they traveled. She was a wonderful wife to Abram. She possessed a grace and beauty that became more refined with age. She knew how to work hard and prepare all that was needed for the caravan, and though she was a simple woman, she was very beautiful. But Sarai didn't focus on her outward beauty, adorning herself with jewels and expensive clothing. Instead, she was known for her unfading inner beauty; her gentle and quiet spirit. She loved Abram and there was no doubt about it. She obeyed Abram, willing to do everything he asked of her. She respected Abram, calling him her lord, and she knew beyond a shadow of doubt that Abram loved and adored her with all his heart.

Once there, Abram set up camps in Canaan and in neighboring areas. He continued to move south as the Lord directed. God once again appeared to Abram showing him how much land He was giving to Abram and his household. Abram traveled the area in stages, setting up camps as he went. At that same time, a severe famine swept over the land of Canaan, forcing Abram to go down to Egypt to live temporarily where there would be provision for all in his household. When the entourage approached the border of Egypt, Abram put his hand on Sarai's, pulling her attention from the task at hand. He looked deep into her eyes.

"You are so beautiful, Sarai."

"Oh, Abram, you need to stop. After all these years, you still think I'm beautiful?"

"Even more so than when we were first married!"

"You are quite the charmer, Abram." Sarai smiled, but as she basked in the memories of when they first wed, her smile faded as reality surfaced. They had been together for decades and still no children were born of their union. She looked up at her husband with love and regret, with tenderness and shame.

"What's wrong my love?"

"I have let you down, my lord. I have not been able to give you a son. I have not been an instrument used by God to fulfill His promises to you. I'm afraid that it will never happen for us, that you will become tired of me and reach out for another woman who can be a vessel of inheritance for you."

"Oh, Sarai, how could I ever love another? Besides, there's no need to worry. God will do as He has promised."

Even though Abram sounded confident, Sarai was less sure. It was evident that she was not yet a believer in this fulfillment, but she loved her husband and did not want him to see her doubting God.

"I'm sure you're right, my dear husband," Sarai said, trying to convince him that she believed what he said. She attempted to push aside her doubt and fear, smiling at Abram so as not to make him worry. He smiled back, taking in the view of his beautiful wife sitting next to him.

"You are so beautiful, Sarai, not just outwardly, but you possess the inner beauty of a queen. We will have children, as the Lord promised. What I am concerned about now, though, is that someone in Egypt will see your beauty and try to take you away from me. They might even kill me to have you." Sarai was quiet as she considered what Abram had said. Could he be serious or was the desert's heat having an affect on him?

The breeze from the desert cooled the sweat that streamed down Abram's forehead as he wondered what lie ahead of them. *Would he be able to keep his entourage safe? Would he be able to meet the demands of food and supplies needed to maintain his household?* He thought about the unknowns he would meet as he entered Egypt, a land with princes and armies. How would he keep Sarai safe as he headed for a nation he had not been to before? Abram felt the need to stress to Sarai the importance of not disclosing that they were married. So he broached the subject again.

"Sarai, promise me that you will tell anyone who approaches you that you are my sister."

"Don't be silly, Abram, I will do no such thing."

"No, Sarai, really, I'm serious, it's not safe. Please, promise that you will tell them you are my sister."

"Of course, my lord, I will do as you say and tell them that I am your sister, but I really think you are worrying about nothing. Who would want me? I am old and barren," she insisted. But Abram knew differently. He knew others would be overtaken by his wife's undeniable beauty!

Abram's humanity was evident. Even though he trusted that God's promises would come true, he was fearful of what could happen to him in Egypt. To protect himself, he conspired with Sarai and lied on two occasions about her being his sister instead of his wife. Unfortunately, he was setting a bad example for Sarai by not trusting God to protect him. And yet, God showered His grace on them, protecting Sarai and Abram in their travels.

As Abram and Sarai sojourned through Egypt and arrived in King Abimelech's kingdom, they lied about their relationship when they spoke with the king. They did not tell the king that they were married. The king was so taken with Sarai's beauty that he added Sarai to His harem. As a result of taking Abram's wife, the king, his wives, and his concubines experienced infertility. It was only after a warning and correction from God in a dream that King Abimelech released Sarai from his harem and sent her and Abram out of his kingdom. Heeding the call of God, Abram prayed for Him to restore the fertility of the king and the women in his harem.

And God did.

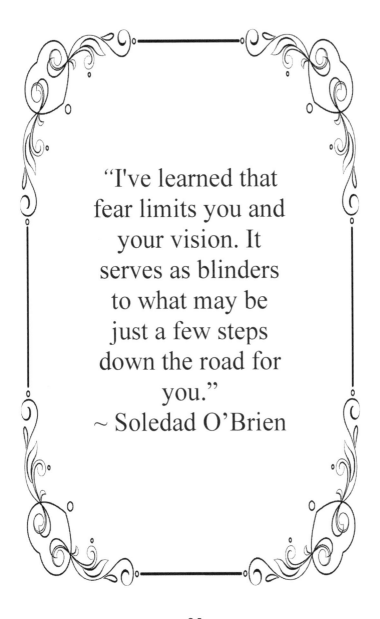

"I've learned that fear limits you and your vision. It serves as blinders to what may be just a few steps down the road for you."
~ Soledad O'Brien

DOUBT

*"What strength do I have that I should
continue to hope?
What is my future, that I should be patient?"*
Job 6:11 CSB

Sarai's life hadn't changed much after marrying Abram. The most significant adjustments involved a change of address. They had moved a couple times in obedience to God's instructions. But the status of her family life had not changed…there was still no child.

Sarai felt stuck in life. She may have thought, "Things are so hard right now. It feels like God is not hearing my cries of anguish. Is He really on my side? How can I have hope for a breakthrough and give Abram a son—the heir he desires?" She was steadily losing hope in the promise God had made to Abram about having innumerable descendants.

But hope, according to 1 Corinthians 13:13, is one of three eternal things that allows us to tap into God's grace. We are to *always* have hope. Hope is not just a wish. Bible lexicons define hope as *the joyful and confident expectation of good.* To live with hope means you have a genuine and confident expectancy of good in your life! In other words, you're always expecting that God *will* do what He said He would do.

In stressful times of life when you feel stuck between a rock and a hard place, it can be difficult to hope that things will get better. Distractions come to take your focus off of God's love and His faithfulness to His Word. That's what happened to Sarai. Her long-term barrenness distracted her. Sarai was losing hope that she would ever give birth to Abram's heir. She put her trust in her circumstances more than in God's promises. God said they would have a child through whom many generations would be blessed. But the promise no longer mattered much to Sarai because the anguish she felt had turned her trust into doubt.

Although Sarai was a woman who possessed great inner strength, she gave in to the thoughts that *she* must make things happen if Abram was to ever have a biological heir. While Sarai was waiting on God to do what He had promised, she became impatient and devised her own solution. Doubting God's promises, Sarai suggested to her husband that he should have a child through a surrogate, her slave Hagar. By giving up on God's promise, Sarai showed that she was willing to relinquish her position as the promised biological matriarch... to a slave!

Sarai found herself in agony. She was devastated that she could not provide Abram with a son, the one thing that would bring him comfort and joy and fulfill God's promise.

Birthing a son was beyond her control. In their culture, only women who could birth children were considered whole. She felt incomplete, a failure, a cursed woman, seemingly punished for sins unknown. She most likely questioned, "If God had a plan, why was I not a part of it?" So, she went to the Source, God, and had a conversation with Him while she and Abram were in Canaan.

"Lord, because Abram was so distraught, I believe You gave him that vision about a multitude of descendants for encouragement. He was so excited when he came home and told me all about it. He said You told him not to be afraid, that You would protect him. I could tell he had been uneasy before he met with You, I could see it in his eyes. It's too bad that he doubted You would protect him. He regretted having done so. But that's not the thing that is on his heart. Lord, he wants a son. He doesn't want to live with the shame of not being blessed by You. He doesn't want to have to leave his wealth to Eliezer, his servant, simply because he has no son of his own.

He believes Your promises are true—he believes in You, Lord. His desire, though, is to leave a legacy, to have an heir who would inherit all You have given him. I know he may appear to doubt You, but He loves You Lord. His heart is heavy because he feels he let You down. After all, it's been 10 years since your first promise to him. So I'm sure that's why You took him outside and showed him the stars. That was enough for him. He looked up into the sky and saw the immense presence of Your creation. You promised him that his descendants would become as vast as the stars in the sky. Then You cemented that promise with a covenant ceremony.

That was enough for Abram, Lord. That encouraged his faith. But what about me? Where does that leave me? What would You have me to do? I am still barren. We've been here 10 years in this land you sent us to, but still, I have not been able to give Abram a son." Sarai paused and hesitantly rubbed her belly, as if longing for a child would make a baby appear. "Where does that leave me, Lord? What about me? Am I not a part of Your promise? I can't stand to see Abram this way. I can't handle not being able to give him a son. How long, Lord, will it be like this? I feel devastated." Tears welled up in her eyes. She was not sure that God would keep His promise.

"Your message seemed to encourage Abram, but it has left me feeling hopeless and broken-hearted. I know he heard You say that You will make him the father of many nations, but was there anything in there about me? Why do I remain barren, Lord? Why have You cursed me? Why have You prevented me from having children? What have I done to deserve this? What have I done, Lord? *Please* tell me, what have I done?"

Sarai felt as if she was cursed, but in her heart she knew that was not the case.

She broke down sobbing and curled up on the floor. She was overwhelmed by God's silence, by the sheer reality that she had not conceived a child in spite of the fact that a promise had been made to her husband, Abram.

Sarai was exhausted from crying. She removed the headscarf she was wearing, rolled it into a ball, and tucked it under her head for a pillow. As she lay quietly, she began to wonder if she was not the one to be used to fulfill God's promise to Abram. "You made that promise to him, that he will have a son of his own who would be his heir. God, you specifically told him that he would not see this promise fulfilled through his servant, but through himself." She pondered even more. She did not want to get in God's way. But what was her part in all of this? How could she make God's promise a reality? Sarai thought and thought. God was not answering her questions. She began to wonder if He even heard her. She thought about all of the women in their household and how they were having babies and growing families.

"Lord, it's just not fair that the master's wife cannot have children." And with that, Sarai wept even more. When she had no more tears to cry, the thought came to her that the servant women in their household *were* having babies.

"What if I had a servant carry Abram's child for me? What if I gave my servant Hagar to Abram to bear children? God, is that your answer? If I give Hagar to Abram as a wife, could she bare sons for me?" she wondered aloud.

Sarai gave a sigh of relief, not waiting for God to answer, but thinking that would be how she could make God's plan a reality.

"Yes, that must be it. After all, Hagar is of childbearing age and as my servant, she will do whatever I ask of her. Hagar could surely have sons for me!"

The more Sarai thought about it, the more she liked the idea. It would be simple and God's promise to Abram would be fulfilled.

"Yes, that is what I will do. I will present Hagar to him as a wife and she will fulfill God's promise to Abram, and he will have sons." And so it was settled. Sarai would give Hagar to Abram as a wife to begin the family that Sarai had not been able to produce on her own.

Sarai approached Abram with her idea of how they could make the seemingly impossible possible.

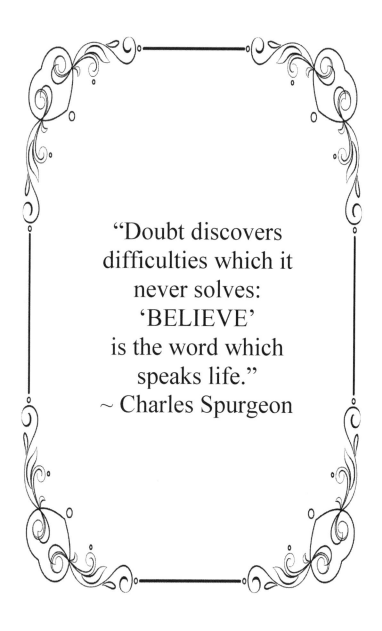

"Doubt discovers
difficulties which it
never solves:
'BELIEVE'
is the word which
speaks life."
~ Charles Spurgeon

ANGER

"So Sarai said to Abram, 'The Lord has prevented me from having children. Go and sleep with my servant. Perhaps I can have children through her.' And Abram agreed with Sarai's proposal." **Genesis 16:2 NLT**

Sarai made some poor choices under the influence of doubt. The level of her mistrust about God's promise of a son continued to increase. Doubt clouded her judgment because it was taking so long for her to see the manifestation of the son God had promised them. Sarai made a decision to help God accelerate His promise. The details of that decision, and the consequences of it, turned out not to be anywhere close to what she desired.

Doubting God's goodness and His faithfulness to keep His word, she offered her slave, Hagar, to Abram. It was customary of that time that any child conceived by a slave would belong to the master. So, Sarai decided to have her husband impregnate Hagar so that the slave could produce the child that Abram so terribly wanted.

Because Abram trusted Sarai, he agreed to take Hagar as a wife. He was confident Sarai had a part in God's promise, but he too was desperate to see it come to pass. He wanted to believe that this was the way God had meant it to be all along. He lay with Hagar and she became pregnant. Abram was filled with joy!

In the beginning, Sarai was filled with that same joy. She was basking in the idea that she would soon produce a child for Abram, through her servant Hagar. Sarai catered to Hagar, making sure she was eating well and taking rests throughout the day. She watched as Hagar began to show, thinking God's promise was finally coming to pass — Abram would have descendants just as God had promised. But as Hagar's stature grew physically, so did her sense of entitlement. After all, she was about to birth the master's child.

This truth made Hagar emboldened. Hagar's sense of increased importance was noticed around the camp. Hagar began to be viewed differently among the other handmaidens. She was no longer just a servant; she was now a wife of Abram and revered by others. Hagar commanded her rightful place as one of Abram's wives. It wasn't long before she started to challenge Sarai's authority. No longer taking orders from Sarai, she used the excuse that she was with child and needed to rest.

Handmaidens of the household began taking up her slack; she even gave a few of them orders herself, totally usurping Sarai's authority. At first, Sarai ignored the subtle hints of Hagar's rebellion, but after a while, Sarai began to resent Hagar's presence. With the pregnancy of Hagar, the servant girls looked at Sarai differently. Barrenness was considered a defect, and in their eyes it made Sarai less than a woman. As was the custom in those days, they saw her barrenness as a curse: a punishment from God.

To add insult to injury, Hagar was going around camp acting as if she was the important one and Sarai was insignificant. As a wife of the master, Hagar took advantage of her status. Sarai could feel the glares and hear the whispers as she walked past the servants. She now felt despised and disrespected; it was as if a plague had attached itself to her. She thought she was a disappointment to Abram — that she was no longer needed; a worthless burden. Using a surrogate for Abram's baby was not supposed to go this way. This was not Sarai's plan at all.

Sarai's plan was to provide a child, an heir to Abram, and become the "mother of many nations." But now things were very different. It didn't appear that it would happen as she imagined. Little by little, Hagar was pushing Sarai out of the way. In Sarai's eyes, Hagar was still her servant— commanded to provide children for her master, Abram. But Hagar saw things very differently. She was doing what Sarai could not, and even though Abram had not chosen Hagar, she knew that now that she was with child, things could quickly change. She could take the place of the favorite wife, adding more and more children to Abram's household. This fact did not escape Sarai either.

As time passed and Hagar's belly grew, Sarai detected a gleam in Abram's eye as he watched Hagar walk past. Sarai could see the pride Hagar had as she smiled and flirted with

Abram, returning his glance. Hagar filled Abram with excitement and the hope of a son, something that Sarai had not been able to do. The mere thought of Hagar having even more children with Abram brought Sarai to her breaking point. Having her children was one thing, but taking her man was quite another.

As Sarai observed the unfolding new interaction between Abram and Hagar, jealousy gripped her heart. Even if Abram was unaware of Hagar's intentions, Hagar knew exactly what she was doing. Sarai once again, took matters into her own hands. Approaching Hagar, Sarai commanded,

"Hagar, Abram is hungry. Go and prepare him an afternoon meal."

Hagar replied, "I am sure Abram would not want his wife who is bearing his child to tire herself by preparing a meal for him. Being with child makes me feel tired and exhausted. Why don't you prepare it, my lady, for you cannot make that same claim?"

"That was not a suggestion, Hagar. Abram needs something to eat now, as well as the other men that are harvesting the grain. Please do not delay."

Hagar was now defiant. She looked at Sarai with contempt and then down at her growing belly as if to imply that she was in no condition to work.

"You will do as I have asked, Hagar. You work for me and I am telling you what I need!"

"Well, my lady, I am too exhausted and I will not be able to prepare the meal. Maybe one of the other servant girls will help you. I'm sure they will take care of whatever you ask. Or, if you're finding that they don't listen like they used to, I can ask one of them for you. They seem to do whatever I ask them to do. Besides, the master would not want me to do anything that would jeopardize our child. I saw the way he looked at me today. He seems so pleased that I will soon give him the son that you were unable to give him. You would not want to injure my master's child would you? I'm sorry that you are cursed, but I am here now. My master will not have to worry about God's promise being fulfilled any longer. You have made him wait all these years but I am giving him a son immediately. You really should find a way to make yourself useful."

With that, Hagar started to walk away. Noticing Sarai's look of shock, Hagar stopped to add insult to injury.

"Oh, never mind, that is an impossible task for you, I know. I will ask one of the servant girls to prepare the meal for my master," Hagar replied in a condescending tone. Then she continued to walk towards the well where the other women were gathered.

Sarai was numb. She did not know how to reply. At first she wanted to lash out at Hagar, but she quickly acknowledged inwardly that Hagar was right, so she did the only thing she thought she could do; she let Hagar walk away. Ignoring the biting remarks had become her normal response to Hagar these past couple of months. But now Hagar had taken it too far. This treatment of contempt had been the most belligerent confrontation the two women had experienced. Sarai hurried to her tent where she could fold in defeat privately; she allowed her mind to carry her to a dark place.

Sarai barely spoke in a whisper to herself. "All that Hagar said is true. I have been cursed by God. I can't see where I am personally a part of God's plan at all. My servants treat me differently since Hagar's pregnancy, and I have to rely on Hagar to do what I cannot — have a son for Abram." Sarai sank into a sea of pity and despair as the battle in her mind continued.

"Why did Abram ever choose me for his wife? Was it to bring me to this point of shame and guilt?"

Sitting on a mat on the floor of her tent, Sarai bent her head in anguish and defeat and she sobbed. From deep within she could feel the pain welling up. She cried, and heaved, crawling into a ball in the corner of her dwelling.

"I witnessed Abram's admiration for Hagar," Sarai began to imagine, noting he had never looked at her with such anticipation before. It was more than she could handle.

"Why, Lord, could I not be the one to fulfill Your promise to Abram? Why can I not be the 'mother of many nations'?"

After some time, Sarai lay still on the tent floor, as she thought about the many years of marriage with Abram. They had been together as husband and wife for decades and still no child. The journey in her mind brought her through emotional peaks and valleys. One moment she smiled as she remembered their younger days and the dreams and plans they had made. The next moment she sulked at the thought of the disappointment that filled their lives over and over again each month as they waited for a sign of hope.

After laying there for what seemed like an eternity, Sarai's thoughts again went to Hagar and her despair was replaced with anger, but no longer at Hagar. Now Sarai's indignation turned towards her husband. After all, it was Abram's fault that Hagar was pregnant. Sarai's imagination continued to run away with her and soon she became Abram's accuser, judge, and jury. The question now was, "What had Abram done?"

Yes, indeed, what had he done and why had he looked at Hagar in that way? Why did Abram agree to take Hagar as his wife? He was so quick to lay with her. Was this what he had secretly wanted all along? After all, Hagar was much younger than Sarai and so beautiful and physically appealing.

The more Sarai entertained these thoughts, the more she found herself in an even lower emotional pit. She could no longer hold it in. As the thoughts continued to swirl around in her mind, anger welled up inside. With no room to contain her emotions, the anger came spilling out from her thoughts of rage. Sarai may not have had all the answers, but one thing was clear, she would not have been treated like this had Abram not demanded to sleep with Hagar. Anger and bitterness were now brewing in Sarai's heart disguised as feelings of hurt and betrayal. Sarai would settle this once and for all she thought, and she marched over to the place where Abram was working. Taking Abram aside, she unleashed what she could no longer hold in.

"Why did you sleep with her?" Sarai demanded.

"Sleep with who, Sarai? What are you talking about?" Abram questioned with a puzzled look on his face.

"Hagar! Who else would I be talking about?" Sarai yelled.

"What is all of this about, Sarai? You came to me with Hagar and we agreed. Sleeping with Hagar was your idea, not mine," Abram said in even tones trying to defuse her hostility.

Speaking angrily and out of breath, Sarai continued.

"Well, you didn't have to show her favor! You didn't have to treat her special! And now that she's pregnant, she treats me with contempt, and it's all your fault! If you did not make her think she was special, this would not be happening. If you did not gaze at her as she strutted past you, she wouldn't feel you desired her over me. If you hadn't slept with her, she would still believe herself to be my servant. See, this is all your fault and God will be the judge between us as to who is right!" Sarai felt emboldened with those words and she now looked at her husband indignantly, waiting for him to reestablish her status as his true wife.

Abram remained silent, not knowing what to say. He was hurt and astonished that Sarai felt this way. It wasn't for love that he slept with Hagar, for he truly loved Sarai. He believed God but deeply trusted his wife when she said that the Lord had prevented her from having children. Abram honored Sarai's request to sleep with her handmaiden, believing that through Hagar God's promise would be accomplished. He wanted to please Sarai as much as she wanted to please him.

At first Abram had been confident that God would do as He had promised, but Abram allowed his compassion for his wife to overtake his better judgment, and now he was in a hard place. He chose his words carefully as he replied to Sarai.

"She was your servant when you gave her to me and she is still your servant. I will not further complicate things — do with her as you please! You are the wife of my youth and I love you. I wash my hands of this." And with that, Abram kissed her forehead and returned to work.

With those words spoken by her husband, Sarai felt empowered in her feelings and justified in the actions she was about to take. She took this opportunity to let Hagar know how she felt.

"I know you feel special Hagar, but Abram reminded me you are my servant before you are his wife. You will do as I ask, with child or not. And I will no longer tolerate you usurping my authority or disobeying my orders. I am your master and you are my servant!"

Hagar was forced to return to her life as a servant. No longer having an elevated status among the other women in the camp, she was now the one being treated with contempt by Sarai. Since she had been put in her place, the handmaidens were fearful to accommodate Hagar. Sarai treated her so harshly that soon after their encounter Hagar ran away.

Sarai felt relieved—she was finally rid of Hagar and that child which was going to be born.

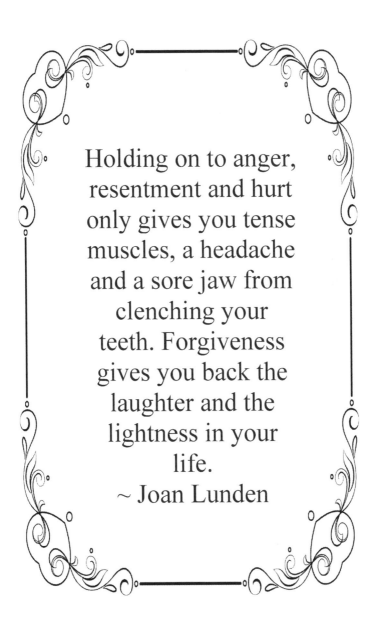

Holding on to anger,
resentment and hurt
only gives you tense
muscles, a headache
and a sore jaw from
clenching your
teeth. Forgiveness
gives you back the
laughter and the
lightness in your
life.
~ Joan Lunden

HOPE

"Even when there was no reason for hope, Abraham [Abram] kept hoping—believing that he would become the father of many nations. For God had said to him, 'That's how many descendants you will have!'"

Romans 4:18 NLT

In response to Sarai's accusations about his responsibility for the difficulties with Hagar, Abram decided to give the slave surrogate back to Sarai. He wanted nothing to do with the territorial fight between Sarai and Hagar. Because Sarai's mistreatment of Hagar was so harsh, it left Hagar with no one to turn to and nowhere to go. She left Abram's household and fled into the wilderness to hide. But can anyone truly ever hide from God?

We're not given many details about Hagar's

wilderness experience except this one major event—she had an encounter with God. Knowing that God saw her pain and heard her cries strengthened Hagar.

After having walked a long time, Hagar became tired. She paused to rest beside a spring of water, hoping to gather her thoughts as well as refresh herself. How could this have happened? Here she was, pregnant with Abram's child, yet destined to live without friends and family and isolated from all she had known. Alone in the wilderness, she wept in anguish.

Hagar sat as she thought and wondered where to go from here. There was no one in the desert to care for her or help her through the delivery. She wondered if Abram would even notice she was gone. If she hadn't treated Sarai so poorly she would still be in the camp. The camp offered protection, food and shelter, and people that cared about her. Now she had nothing.

A cool breeze blew in the shade of the trees at the spring of water where Hagar was resting. At this oasis in the wilderness, where she was regaining her strength, the angel of the Lord found Hagar sitting alone. The angel approached and called her by name.

"Hagar, Sarai's servant, where have you come from, and to where are you going?" It was not that the angel was unaware of Hagar's troubles and travels, but it was for Hagar's benefit that he spoke out, letting her know that God not only knew where she was, but also, who she was.

Hagar was startled by the appearance of the visitor, but she was not frightened. She wondered to herself why someone would come to find her in the wilderness. Suddenly, aware of her position, Hagar felt ashamed of her actions back at the camp.

"I'm running away from my mistress, Sarai, who tormented me and treated me harshly, even though I am carrying her child for her," she replied.

The angel of the Lord caught her gaze, and looking straight into her eyes, said to her, "Return to your mistress, and submit to her authority." Those words cut like a knife into the very being of Hagar. The angel continued: "Now that you are pregnant, you will give birth to a son and you are to name him Ishmael, meaning 'God hears.' The Lord has heard your cries of pain and seen your heartbreak.

This son of yours will be as wild as an untamed donkey! He will be against everyone, and everyone will be against him. He will live in open hostility against all his relatives."

Hagar sat transfixed by the words the angel spoke. She could feel that the angel told the truth. She was amazed that God would seek her out in the wilderness, give her His promise of a future, and pave a way for her to go back home. She would not have to live in the desert alone, raising a child with no sustenance and no one to care for them.

While she listened, a look of embarrassment crept over her face as she inwardly acknowledged she had behaved shamefully towards Sarai and disrespectfully towards Abram. But even in her shameful actions, the Lord found her right where she was, wandering in the wilderness, both physically and spiritually.

Hagar replayed the angel's message in her mind. The God of the universe saw her! He sent a messenger into the wilderness to find her. At that moment, Sarai did not matter to Hagar; Abram did not matter. Not even the angel's somewhat negative report about a son named Ishmael mattered. What did matter was that God knew who *she* was! Those were the only words Hagar heard and held on to. Everything the angel said after that was lost in the hope that now filled her heart. God's words gave Hagar great hope. Even though the angel had said difficult things, those words were not her focus. She had hope because she realized God saw her.

She held on to the assurance that she could go home. She felt a renewed sense of purpose. She had heard from God himself and God had named her child. Peace replaced the dismay that had flooded Hagar's soul now that she knew she was not alone. Hagar recognized that the hand of God was upon her and she responded to Him, "You are El-roi, the God who sees me."

Hagar was so touched by God and yet, bewildered as to why He would seek her out. With a full heart, she questioned, "Have I truly seen the One who sees me?" But the peace in her spirit assured her she had. This encounter left her more confident and strong enough to face Sarai's wrath again. She was instilled with courage to go back to Abram and Sarai's camp to give birth to Ishmael. The experience was so impactful that she named the nearby source of water, "Well of the Living One Who Sees Me". Hagar then returned to Abram's camp, confident that God was with her.

In His grace, God granted Hagar the unusual privilege of being spoken to by one of His angels. This stands as a testimony to justice on Hagar's behalf, indicating both Sarai and Abram had used her to force God's promise to happen. God promised Hagar a son and He delivered on His promise. Hagar gave birth to Ishmael when Abram was 86 years old.

What must Sarai have thought about God upon Hagar's return? Did Sarai possibly wonder if God had seen *her* pain and heard *her* cries? Her decision to follow through on her doubt-inspired ideas had backfired. She was not happy that Abram now had a son through another woman. She was not pleased that Abram finally had a legitimate heir. Doubting God's promise did not lead to anything but more unhappiness. How was she to have hope that the four of them, Abram, Sarai, Hagar, and Ishmael, could live a peaceable and satisfying life together?

But was Abram's first-born son, Ishmael, the fulfillment of what God had promised in the covenant He had made with Abram? Apparently not! God made it clear that Abram's covenantal legacy was not through Ishmael but through a son yet to be born. Most importantly, that son was to come through Sarai, not a surrogate.

No matter her intentions, Sarai had gotten ahead of God. She had lost hope and tried to do everything in her *own* power and timing to have a child. Even though Sarai thought God was taking too long and needed her assistance, God still wanted to keep His promise to Abram and Sarai. This led to God giving each of them a new name.

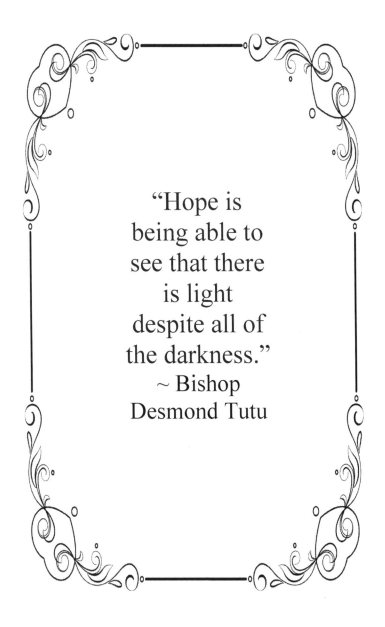

"Hope is
being able to
see that there
is light
despite all of
the darkness."
~ Bishop
Desmond Tutu

FAITH

"Because of faith, Sarah herself received physical power to conceive a child, even when she was long past the age for it, because she considered God Who had given her the promise to be reliable and true to His word."
Hebrews 11:11 AMPC

Whenever God changed a person's name in the Bible, it was to proclaim and establish a new identity for that person. These names were given as a declaration and confirmation of their destiny. In the instance of Abram and Sarai, they had previously exhibited a lack of trust that God would fulfill His promise of a son. God gave them a more permanent reminder of His covenant. He chose to change their names to Abraham and Sarah. By doing so, He gave them assurance that He would still work His plan for them despite their doubts, fears, and actions. The new names acted as a seal to the covenant, seeds for His plan, and a sign of His purpose. With the name change, they entered a new state of grace.

Abram entered Sarai's tent with that youthful glow she had seen at other times in their marriage, usually after he had an encounter with God. He was smiling and seemed to gaze out into the distance as if he could see something no one else could see. "I know that look, Abram. You seem so preoccupied. What is on your mind today?" she questioned.

He confidently responded, "It's going to happen just as God said it would. I *will* be a father of many nations."

"It's been thirteen years since God blessed you with a son, but only one son. Where is His promise to you? Where are the many nations of descendants? Is it that Ishmael will father many sons?" Sarai questioned her husband. This did not make sense to Sarai. God had always been a God of His word, but what was going on? And where was His promise to her, she wondered?

"My name is no longer Abram," he said. "God has changed it to Abraham, which means father of many nations! And your name is no longer Sarai, for God has re-named you. Your name is now Sarah, the mother of many nations. You will have a son and kings will be your descendants." Abraham was grinning from ear to ear as he became more and more animated about his exciting encounter.

"God appeared to me today, Sarah," Abram began, "and at first...at first, even I laughed, for I am way too old to father a child. But God specifically said you will be the mother of my son. *You* Sarah!" He caught her by her arm and pulled her close. "This is what we've been waiting for Sarah! This is it!"

Sarah was not so convinced. She had heard this for many years and yet nothing had happened.

"Why would God wait until I was past the age of bearing children to tell me that I would be the mother of many nations; that kings of nations would be my descendants? Why could I not have been personally told this before— before Hagar and Ishmael?"

"You did hear it before, Sarah! You heard it from me and I heard it from God. But we did not wait for His promise to be fulfilled. We rushed in and made it happen on our own. It wasn't God's fault!"

Sarah looked down in embarrassment. Abraham was right. It had been her idea to use Hagar as the surrogate. Sarah felt ashamed of her impatience. She wanted to believe that this was it, that now would be the time that God was going to fulfill His promise, but she was fearful and did not want to experience yet another disappointment. She resolved to wait and see what the Lord was going to do.

A short time later, the Lord appeared again to Abraham. It was at that time that Sarah had her own encounter with God. She was in the tent one day when Abraham ran inside, excited and out of breath.

"Sarah, hurry! I need you to get three large measures of your best flour to knead into dough to bake some bread." Abraham was swiftly moving all around the tent, grabbing utensils and spices, turning here and there. "Sarah, where is the, the…" He paused as he looked around. "Oh what is it called?"

"What are you talking about, Abraham, and why are you out of breath and running around the tent?" Sarah couldn't imagine what had Abraham so excited.

"We have some visitors and I've invited them to stay and rest awhile as I prepare a meal for them. They have been traveling and I know they are tired and hungry," Abraham responded as he hurried around the tent gathering the tools he would need to prepare the meal.

"Who are these guests, Abraham?" Sarah asked inquisitively as she also began to move a little quicker around the tent doing as Abraham had asked.

"It is the Lord and his servants, Sarah. The Lord! And they have stopped here before they travel to Sodom."

Sarah stopped in her tracks, unsure of the words that had just come out of Abraham's mouth. She inquired, "The Lord? The Lord is *here*? Abraham, have you been drinking? You know it is much too early in the day to have been drinking."

Abraham stopped long enough to gently grab her shoulders and look into her eyes to say, "No Sarah, I have not been drinking." Then he let her go and continued to work. Sarah could tell by the sound of Abraham's voice that he was serious.

She began moving more quickly and feeling a little excited herself. But then, conviction and guilt set in. The thought of her past instantly crept into her mind. She thought back to her hasty decision to have Hagar sleep with Abraham and she became concerned.

"Why would he come here, Abraham?" Sarah asked awkwardly.

She began to worry that maybe the Lord had come to punish her, or maybe even to confront her about her actions.

"I don't know why but He is here, Sarah, He is!" Abraham said it with such excitement that Sarah could feel the anticipation. Abraham was full of joy, the way he was every time he met with the Lord. He glanced back at Sarah, smiled at her, and then ran out of the tent and towards the herd to choose a tender calf to prepare. Sarah felt both exhilarated and fearful as she continued to prepare the meal. She gathered some yogurt and some milk to be served along with the roasted meat. She couldn't help but think about reasons the Lord would be here, in their camp, at this time. Sarah peeked through the colored fabric of the tent door to catch a glimpse of the visitors, being careful not to be seen. Their backs were to her and she couldn't gaze upon their faces. She couldn't gaze upon *His* face.

When the food was ready, the servant brought the calf and Abraham picked up the food from the tent and hurried out to serve his guests. It was customary for women to serve the men, but Sarah couldn't bring herself to come out of the tent. The visitors and Abraham were sitting under a tree near the oak grove belonging to Mamre as Sarah peered through the fabric once again. She did not want to be seen so she stood behind the layers of the curtain that had been pulled to cover the tent's entrance. She turned her ear towards the guests. From inside the tent, she listened intently as Abraham conversed with the special guests. She was eavesdropping and pondering their conversation as the Lord reaffirmed His promise to Abraham and mentioned her name.

"Where is Sarah, your wife?" the visitors inquired, asking why it was Abraham doing the serving. Sarah moved slightly away from the curtain, not wanting to make it move and reveal her presence. She was surprised that the Lord was asking about her. She wondered quietly to herself if He really did care about her, "Was the Lord really inquiring about me?" She was excited that He had called her by name. But as she thought about what was happening, reasoning set in, changing hope to disbelief.

Not disbelief in God's ability to consider her, but in the mere fact that He *would*. Conversations that Abraham had in the past with the Lord were directly about him, but now He was asking about her.

"She's inside the tent," Abraham replied as his eyes glanced toward the closed curtain of her domain.

The Lord smiled as he glanced towards the tent, then He said to Abraham with confidence, "I will return to you about this time next year and your wife, Sarah, will have a son!"

Sarah was listening attentively with anticipation, but when she heard the statement that she would have a son next year this time, she laughed silently to herself. The thought of her and Abraham having children was amusing to Sarah as they were both very old and past the natural point of conceiving.

"How could a worn-out woman like me enjoy such pleasure? And Abraham is much too old to produce a child," she mused to herself in a ridiculing whisper.

Then the Lord asked Abraham, "Why did Sarah laugh?" Abraham looked at the Lord with bewilderment, because he had heard nothing.

"Why did she say, 'How could a worn out woman like me enjoy such pleasure as having a baby?'" The Lord looked at Abraham with loving eyes and asked, "Is anything too hard for the Lord?" Abraham sat stunned, not able to respond. The Lord continued, "When I return next year about this time, Sarah will have a son."

Sarah was even more shocked than Abraham. How could the Lord have heard her? She was afraid of what that could mean for her and she denied the accusation, whispering in her head, "I did not laugh."

But again the Lord could hear even her thoughts and He replied, "No, you did laugh."

Sarah again stood dumbfounded, ashamed, and embarrassed. How could He have heard her? "He truly is the Lord!" she declared in her heart.

Then the men got up from their meal and continued on their way to Sodom. From that day on, Sarah had a new perspective on God's promises, for she had heard for herself God's specific plan for and about her. She began to see herself as her new name described her "mother of many". Ultimately, the name gave her confidence, and by hearing it over and over again, her faith grew and the unbelievable became believable.

Sarah was almost 90 years old when God declared that she would become pregnant with her first child. This was a declaration of a miracle because Sarah had already gone through menopause. An even more amazing account from Jewish tradition holds that Sarah had no womb at all! This traditional thought is based on the double emphasis in Genesis 11:30, "But Sarai was barren; she had no child." It is believed that this implies that she did not even have a place for offspring— i.e. a womb (Rashi, citing Talmud – Yevamot 64a).

Her pregnancy would have to be a miracle without question. It was to be a result of the hand of God moving in Sarah's life to fulfill His promise. In spite of her barren circumstances and her singular focus on her infertility, God blessed her with renewed youth to look good, feel strong, and become pregnant. But that did not happen right away, or even when Sarah wanted it to. There was much more waiting, anxiety, and hurt before God's promise came to pass.

However, receiving those names, Abraham, which means "father of many nations," and

Sarah, which means "Princess/mother of many," would be life changing for Abraham and Sarah. Their names signified who they were, giving them a new identity that aligned with God's plan. The new names worked to reinforce what God had promised. Their faith in God's promise would be strengthened as they heard themselves and others consistently say these names that would soon determine their destiny.

The names also expressed a new relationship with God and helped Abraham and Sarah understand more clearly how He had lovingly viewed them all along. Their names were prophetic of the blessing they were to experience. This couple could now begin to more fully rely on and depend upon God's strength rather than their own in order to bring about the birth of the promised son. Together, they grew to become a team built on faith.

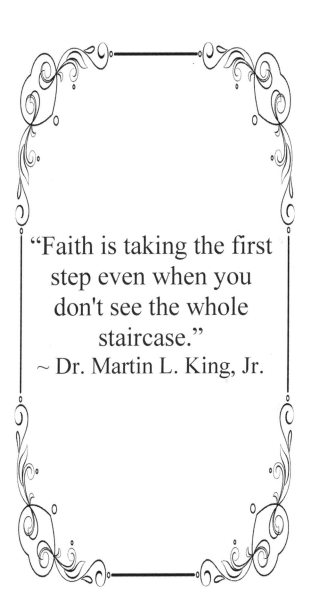

"Faith is taking the first step even when you don't see the whole staircase."
~ Dr. Martin L. King, Jr.

VICTORY

"The Lord kept his word and did for Sarah exactly what he had promised. She became pregnant, and she gave birth to a son for Abraham in his old age. This happened at just the time God had said it would. And Abraham named their son Isaac."
Genesis 21:1-3 NLT

Even though Sarah had been infertile for an extremely long time, God promised Abraham that he would have a multitude of children. He reminded Abraham and Sarah of this promise many times. They were literally hearing, and later experiencing, the Word of God.

And though God repeatedly reminded them of His promise of a child, Sarah still had doubts. Even when God told them specifically *when* the baby would be born, Sarah laughed incredulously at His words and wondered, "Shall I really bear a child when I'm so old?" But, God kept His word and within a year she gave birth.

Standing at the entrance of her tent, Sarah thought to herself as she rubbed her belly. It had been over eleven months since the Lord had visited Abraham and Sarah's camp. Sarah was within earshot when she heard the Lord say she would have a son in a year's time. This amazing promise of God had grown inside Sarah over the past nine months until it had almost come full term, leaving her belly round and firm. The months had gone by fast, filling the camp with excitement over this miraculous event and now it was almost time that Sarah would give birth. She began to sing and praise the Lord for his goodness over the blessing that was springing forth. She paused to talk to the Lord whom she had felt so close to over these past months.

"And Abraham…and Abraham, Lord," Sarah said with a smile. "Lord, he has become giddy with excitement over the prospect of Your promise coming to fruition, even as he turns 100 years old! He's excited like he was during his encounters with You. He is experiencing the completion of Your promise—Your word to him. He doesn't even know how to contain his excitement, Lord. And look what You've done for me. You've brought honor back to my name. The women don't look at me with disdain anymore. I have been the talk of the camp since all of this began and I am so happy. How could I have ever doubted Your word? Please forgive me.

In the beginning I was hopeful, but my hope turned to doubt as the years went by and it was hard for me to stand on a promise You gave to

Abraham alone. But then, Lord," Sarah paused for a moment to ponder His goodness. "Then, Lord, You visited me. You actually made Yourself known to me and You called me by name, letting me know You knew who I was. You let me know that You heard my cries. You even heard my private thoughts." Sarah chuckled as she remembered her thoughts in the tent when the Lord was sitting under the tree.

"You saw me even when I was hiding. And you answered my deepest prayers. There is nothing impossible for You, Lord! You made and kept Your promise to me."

She sat for a moment, stroking her belly and smiling thoughtfully. It was overwhelming and so exciting to Sarah—the promise, the baby, and her husband so full of joy and wonder. How could she have ever doubted God? Everything seemed to be falling into place. Sarah was no longer the spectacle of a woman not being able to conceive. She was now the woman living out God's promise—pregnant in her old age. And then it happened.

While Abraham was out in the field supervising the work of his servants, he saw his Eliezer running towards him.

"Abraham! Abraham! It is happening!" Eliezer said between breaths. As he bent over, placing his hands on his knees to catch his breath, he looked up at Abraham with a smile and said, "Sarah is giving birth! Come quickly, she is with the nursemaids in her tent."

Abraham paused, raised his arms, and looked up to heaven. "Lord, You have delivered on Your promise and I am forever grateful! You are a God of promise; a God of hope, a God of favor, and I love you, Lord." Abraham lowered his arms and ran towards Sarah's tent.

When he arrived, Sarah had already given birth to a beautiful baby boy. After the nursemaids washed and swaddled the baby, Abraham took him in his arms and smiled at the delicate little bundle he was holding. He thought about the years that had passed as he waited for his son of promise. He reminisced about taking Sarah as his wife and the dreams they had dreamt together. He remembered traveling in their first years as they journeyed towards the home God had for them. He thought about the places he and Sarah had visited together. He pondered on the good and the bad they had experienced. It had all culminated into this one point in time—the birth of his son.

Abraham thought about all of the times God had visited with him and promised him that he would be the father of many nations. He remembered his last encounter with God when the Lord told him that he would have a son in a year's time. Abraham was overwhelmed with the love of God. He recalled that God had heard Sarah's thoughts, and he laughed. How shocked she had been to hear God address the very thing she was thinking! She was surprised that God had even heard her silent laugh at the thought that she would conceive a child. That laughter of doubt had now turned into laughter of a promise received, and the promise was resting in Abraham's arms.

"As the Lord commanded, I call you Isaac, little one," Abraham said with laughter in his voice. He looked at Sarah and she laughed with joy too. "Your name means 'he laughs'. Yes, laughter will be your name, and how fitting that is," Abraham boasted as he drew his son in a little closer. "Your mother laughed at the thought she would ever be able to conceive you, and now we both laugh with joy and excitement at your birth." Abraham and Sarah lovingly gazed at each other and then at their precious boy. Abraham basked in the glory of

God just a little longer before he handed Isaac back to Sarah.

Sarah watched Abraham as he beamed at the sight of his son and it brought warmth and gratitude to her heart. She too, remembered all the years with Abraham as she witnessed his unwavering faith. Sarah pulled Isaac to her breast naturally, as if she had done this many times before. She looked down and smiled at her newborn son, her son named Isaac. She declared, "God has brought me laughter and all who hear about this will laugh with me. Who would have said to Abraham that Sarah would nurse a baby? Yet I have given Abraham a son in his old age!"

Sarah was content. She had learned a lot in her 90 years, but most of all she had learned to trust God. She discovered that God really does keep His promises, and the words He gives fulfill all He has commanded—His words never return void.

It took time for Sarah to develop the faith to believe God. It did not happen overnight and it required a lot of shedding of self. She had to give up trying to make things happen in her own strength. She had to give up being in control. It took faith to trust in what God was doing and not circumvent His process. It took faith to let Him be God, and that did not come easily for Sarah. After all, the promise had been made for Sarah to have a child decades before it happened. Only God could make it possible for Sarah to have a child while being barren and in her senior years. Only God! And it did happen. Sarah came to the place where she too believed God would keep His promise.

Because of Sarah's faith, a whole nation came from one man, Abraham, who by all accounts at the age of 100 was considered as good as dead. The promise became a nation with so many people that, as the Scriptures say, it is "like the stars in the sky and the sand on the seashore, there is no way to count." The Lord kept His word and did for Sarah exactly what He had said He would do. Sarah became pregnant and gave birth to a son for Abraham in his old age. This happened at just the time God had said it would.

It's easy for us to slip into doubt. Even though God may be giving us gentle reminders of His promises, we sometimes choose not to hold on until the fulfillment of His Word. When the doubt creeps in, we have to do a self-check and encourage ourselves with what He has promised.

No matter how long we've been facing the problem of infertility, we can still have hope of victory because our circumstances do not limit God. He can be limited only by our unbelief in His willingness to do what He promised. Our hope must be based on the unbreakable covenant promises that God has established. They bring unlimited possibilities to us through the finished work on the cross by His Son, Jesus.

Mark 9:23 states, "All things are possible to him (her) who believes." We can refuse to allow hopelessness to settle into our lives. We can let hope take root and grow in every area of our life, especially regarding getting pregnant and having a healthy baby. We may not always clearly see God doing something in our circumstances but that does not mean that He's not listening to our prayers. Nor does it mean that He does not care about what's happening to us. Sometimes, God is working things out in the background because he knows that our faith needs to be put into action in order for it to grow. No matter what, we can rest assured that He loves us and is on our side. He is always working things out for our good so that we experience victory and live life abundantly.

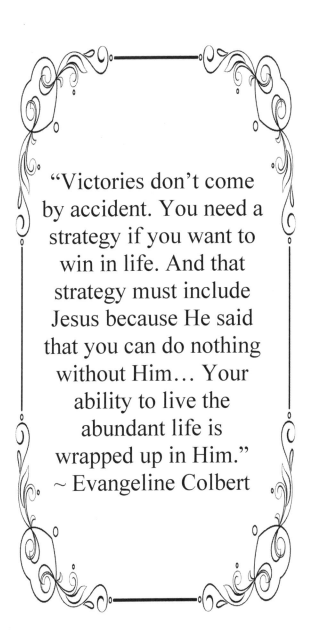

"Victories don't come
by accident. You need a
strategy if you want to
win in life. And that
strategy must include
Jesus because He said
that you can do nothing
without Him… Your
ability to live the
abundant life is
wrapped up in Him."
~ Evangeline Colbert

Profile of a Modern-Day Overcomer

Meet La'Vista, who borrowed hope from Sarah's story:

To say that four plus years of failed pregnancy attempts had taken its toll on me mentally, emotionally, and spiritually, would be an understatement.

I'd gone through multiple tests and treatments, two separate surgeries, various drugs, hormone injections, invasive ultrasounds and Intrauterine Insemination (IUI) to address the unknown cause of my infertility. I had adhered to rigorous ovulation tracking, strict sex schedules with my husband, diet modifications and even naturopathic approaches. I'd prayed earnestly. I shed many heartbroken tears. My faith was pushed to its limits.

With each back-to-back negative pregnancy test, my hope of ever experiencing Motherhood started to diminish.

As the sadness and longing for Motherhood ached within me, I knew that if I didn't deliberately do something to combat the emotional war going on inside of me, I'd eventually lose hope forever.

So when I didn't have enough hope of my own I borrowed it.

I borrowed hope by purposefully reading devotionals that were geared towards infertility. God always met me in His Word and brought me comfort. I borrowed hope by sharing my infertility journey with others. There was something about the commonality of our experiences and seeing their hope that kept my hope alive and gave me the mental fortitude to keep going.

Borrowing hope meant giving others permission to speak hope into my situation. And I had the audacity to believe them when they did! I borrowed hope from my spouse each time he held me, wiped tears from my eyes, and assured me that I was strong enough to keep going and to keep trying. I borrowed hope by standing on the promise of God—that if I took delight in Him, He would give me the desires of my heart. (Psalms 37:4 NIV)

And He did just that. On Monday, August 10, 2015, at 9:09am, "The Cub," my miracle son, made his grand entrance into the world and was placed in my arms. He is my manifested hope and a symbol of hope to many others that are still on their journey.

Even now, when I feel my hope levels dropping, I look at my miracle and I'm reminded that God's promises really are Yes and Amen.
If He did it before, He WILL do it again.

How will *you* borrow hope from Sarah's story?

RECOMMENDED RESOURCES

Check out these resources for further growth and reinforcing your belief in God's promises of fertility.

Find them at www.BooksByEvangeline.com

60-Day Devotional about God's Fertility Promises

How to Maintain Hope in Your Marriage

Thanks From the Authors

Thank you for reading *Sarah's Story*! We hope it encouraged you to keep your hope alive, and showed you that if you don't have enough hope of your own you can borrow hope from someone else's infertility victory.

If you've enjoyed this book, would you please consider giving a review of it on <u>Amazon</u>? Thanks!

Reviews are gold to authors!

Borrowed Hope

A series of books that bring

hope for the waiting womb.

The series features stories of

inCONCEIVABLE power

working amid the struggle of infertility.

Coming Next

Borrowed Hope: Rebekah's Story

Receive an email update

before

Rebekah's Story is released!

Go to: https://bit.ly/2OGI0c7

Connect Online

Fertile Mindset Coaching Services:

www.iHopeCoaching.com

Blog:

www.MakeRoomForMommy.com

Facebook:

www.Facebook.com/hopefilledfocus

 # Hope Notes

_____

_____

_____

_____

_____

_____

_____

_____

_____

_____

_____

_____

_____

_____

_____

_____

_____

_____

_____

_____

_____

_____

_____

_____

_____

Is anything too hard for the Lord?

Genesis 18:14

_____

_____

_____

_____

_____

_____

_____

_____

_____

_____

_____

_____

*Ah, Lord God! Behold, You have made the
heavens and the earth…
nothing is too difficult for You.
Jeremiah 32:17 NASB*

_____

_____

_____

_____

_____

_____

_____

_____

_____

_____

_____

_____

*Behold, I am the Lord, the God of all flesh: is
there any thing too hard for Me?*
Jeremiah 32:27 AMPC

_____

_____

_____

_____

_____

_____

_____

_____

_____

_____

_____

_____

You shall be blessed above all peoples; there
will be no male or female barren
(childless, infertile) among you.
Deuteronomy 7:14 AMP

_____

_____

_____

_____

_____

_____

_____

_____

_____

_____

_____

_____

He will love you and bless you and multiply
you; He will also bless the fruit of your womb.
Deuteronomy 7:13 AMP

28279684R00063